Chicke

Series "Fun Facts on Farm Animals for Kids"

Written by Michelle Hawkins

Chicken

Series "Fun Facts on Farm Animals for Kids"

By: Michelle Hawkins

Version 1.1 ~June 2021

Published by Michelle Hawkins at KDP

Copyright ©2021 by Michelle Hawkins. All rights reserved.

No part of this publication may be reproduced, distributed or transmitted in any form or by any means including photocopying, recording or other electronic or mechanical methods or by any information storage or retrieval system without the prior written permission of the publishers, except in the case of very brief quotations embodied in critical reviews and certain other noncommercial uses permitted by copyright law.

All rights reserved, including the right of reproduction in whole or in part in any form.

All information in this book has been carefully researched and checked for factual accuracy. However, the author and publisher make no warranty, express or implied, that the information contained herein is appropriate for every individual, situation, or purpose and assume no responsibility for errors or omissions.

The reader assumes the risk and full responsibility for all actions. The author will not be held responsible for any loss or damage, whether consequential, incidental, special or otherwise, that may result from the information presented in this book.

All images are free for use or purchased from stock photo sites or royalty-free for commercial use. I have relied on my own observations as well as many different sources for this book, and I have done my best to check facts and give credit where it is due. In the event that any material is used without proper permission, please contact me so that the oversight can be corrected.

There are more Chickens in the world than people.

The Tyrannosaurus Rex is a close relative to the Chicken.

Americans eat more Chicken than beef.

Chickens make more than thirty different sounds.

If an egg sinks in water, it is fresh; if it floats, it is not.

Playing classical music for your Chickens makes for bigger and heavier eggs.

The color of a Chicken eggshell depends on the Chickens' earlobes.

A red ear Chicken produces Brown Eggs.

A fear of Chickens is called Alektorophobia.

Chickens enjoy sleeping high up to avoid predators.

In Egypt, Chickens were known as the Bird that gave Birth every day.

Chickens do not sweat.

A male Chicken is called a Rooster or a Cock.

Chickens dream like humans do.

A mother, Hen, will turn her eggs up to 50 times each day.

An Easter Egger Chicken will lay blue and green eggs.

Mother Hens are teaching their children even before they hatch

Most eggs are laid between 7 to 11 am.

The average life span of a chicken is between five to ten years.

It takes 26 hours for a Hen to produce one egg.

A Chickens body is composed of more water than a human's.

Chickens originated from Asia.

Chickens are considered to be hypoallergenic.

Female baby Chickens are called Pullets before they start laying eggs.

Chickens have bad eyesight at night.

Chickens can taste salt but not sweetness.

Chickens are raised for their meat and eggs.

Free-range Chickens have the best memory.

No matter the shell color, the nutritional value is the same.

Roosters are known for waking people up at dawn.

Chickens recognize people by their faces and voice.

If part of the inside of an egg is cloudy, it means that it is fresh.

Chickens will remember 100 different people and animals.

Chickens know who rules the roost.

A brown egg will cost more than a white egg.

Chickens eat grit to help them break down their food.

Hybrid Chickens will produce over 200 eggs each year.

Chickens have no teeth.

A Silkie Chicken looks like a poodle.

Chickens will lay their eggs in a nest or a nesting box.

Baby Chickens will start to peck at three days.

Chickens enjoy sunbathing.

Chickens will start to pant if they overheat.

The shortest Chicken is the Serama Chicken.

Some Chickens will lay over 250 eggs per year.

It takes 21 days for a chicken egg to hatch.

Chickens make an ideal child's pet.

Baby Chickens are called Chicks.

The 3rd eyelid on a Chicken helps to clean the eye.

Chickens prefer cold weather or hot weather.

A Roosters's job is to look out for predators.

Chickens have 300° vision.

The older the Chicken, the bigger the eggs.

Chickens are omnivores; they eat seeds and insects.

Chickens need at least 14 hours of sunlight to produce eggs.

Baby Chicks come in many different colors, not just yellow.

Chickens are very social.

Chickens have better eyesight than humans during the day.

Chickens that produce brown eggs eat more.

Once a female Chicken lays an egg, they are called a Hen.

Chickens can live up to 25 years in the wild.

Chickens can see the difference in colors better than humans.

In Gainsville, Florida, it is illegal to eat fried Chicken with utensils.

Chickens make great pets.

The scientific name for Chicken is Gallus gallus domesticus.

There are over 175 different types of Chicken in the world.

Birds can fly over a fence.

Chickens only have 350 taste buds; humans have 10,000.

Chickens dream in color.

A group of Chickens is called a flock.

Chickens don't blink.

Chickens need to eat four pounds of food to produce twelve eggs.

The tallest Chicken is the Malay Chicken.

Chickens will eat all types of bugs and insects.

A Chickens heart will beat between 220 to 360 beats per minute.

The skin under a Rooster beak is called a Wattle.

The red skin on a Chickens head is called a comb.

Chickens will cackle when an egg is produced to keep predators away.

There are over 25 billion Chickens in the world.

Cooked beans are fine to feed to Chickens; raw beans can be fatal if eaten.

Chickens will flap their wings to cool down.

Chickens can swim.

Chickens will clean themselves by taking a dust bath.

The wild mushroom Laetiporus tastes just like Chicken.

Find me on Amazon at:

https://amzn.to/3oqoXoG

and on Facebook at:

https://bit.ly/3ovFJ5V

Other Books by Michelle Hawkins

Series

Fun Facts on Birds for Kids.

Fun Fact on Fruits and Vegetables

Fun Facts on Small Animals

Fun Facts on Dogs for Kids.

Fun Facts on Dates for Kids.

Fun Facts on Zoo Animals for Kids

Fun Facts on Farm Animals for Kids.

Printed in Great Britain
by Amazon